AF207668

Praise for

THE HAUNTING OF POTTER'S FIELD

"Evocative and poignant, the storied poems in *The Haunting of Potter's Field* shine a light on the lives of those who were overlooked in past generations, some buried without a name. In this most unusual and beautifully illustrated book, Margaret Shaw Johnson reminds us that those who are 'the forgotten' in the history of our communities deserve room in our collective memory."

Kathleen Kenney Peterson, playwright and author:
Girl on the Leeside and Summer for the Taking.

"With a little spooky fun, Margaret Shaw Johnson sheds light on neglected characters in early Midwestern history. 'Old Mose' in particular is a comic ride and a reminder that great tales can come from surprising places."

Chris Rogers, Winona Post Editor

"Margaret Shaw Johnson is a forensic poet, and in *The Haunting of Potter's Field*, has enriched the penniless, given voice to the long ago silenced, and brought those almost anonymous into the creative limelight. The Midwest and Minnesota now have their own Spoon River Anthology, and these colorful and disparate lives, conjured with wit, love-songs, and laments, are now properly memorialized, to be remembered and cherished. You will forever wander past a Potter's Field and want to enter and explore, especially yours close to home."

Lee Gundersheimer, theatre producer, playwright, performer, and educator, is
currently the Arts and Culture Coordinator for the City of Winona, Minnesota.

"Margaret Shaw Johnson's *The Haunting of Potter's Field* hearkens back to the style and tone of the early twentieth century in *Spoon River Anthology* (1915). Edgar Lee Masters told us the stories of the 'residents' of the local cemetery, many of them prominent citizens. Margaret Shaw Johnson focuses on the community's forsaken and tells us their stories with insight and compassion. Jared Tuttle's artwork adds an edgy gothic element to the text. One is transported to that time and place, and the writing is such that one can't help but read the book out loud"

Ken McCullough, author of Broken Gates, Dark Star, and Left Hand.

"Johnson finds poetry in the stories of the usually unsung among us, those who die penniless and alone, buried in a pauper's grave. Her verse reminds us of the anguish faced by some immigrants in the great migration from Europe and Asia to what is now the U.S. Midwest. For some, the American Dream was a nightmare. Johnson's poems reflect their fate and remind us of the value of human relationships we nurtured during our lives. A memorable read."

Frances Edstrom, Winona Post Editor, retired

"*The Haunting of Potter's Field* is a delight to read. It tells the stories of ordinary but unfortunate people who would otherwise be forgotten. What the author has done should inspire others to search for those stories, as well."

Mark Peterson, former Executive Director of the Winona County
Historical Society and City of Winona Mayor

The Haunting Of Potter's Field

Published by: Ravens Point Press, 719 Main St., Winona, Minnesota USA
Email Contact: Ravenspointpress@gmail.com
Visit: Ravenspointpress.com

Music Score to "Tell Your Story" © 2011 by Brian Schellinger, used with permission.
Email Contact: squatyboy@live.com

Music Score to "Maggie's Lament" © by Kelly McGuire, used with permission.
Email Contact: kmcguire@svdpmarinette.com

Illustrations by:
Jared Tuttle Illustration and Design, LLC
Minneapolis, Minnesota
Email Contact: hello@jared-tuttle.com

Book design by:
Rachel Tesch Hudachek
Email Contact: rachelltesch@gmail.com

Editor: Sandy Sullivan
Ivywild Editing & Writing Services, LLC
Email Contact: sandy@ivywildeditingandwriting.com

Publicist: Rachel Anderson
RMA Publicity
Email Contact: rachel@rmapublicity.com

Identifiers: ISBN 978-1-7360372-0-1
Library of Congress Control Number: 2020921639

Subjects : BISAC: FICTION/Historical/General
LITERARY COLLECTIONS/American/General
HISTORY/United States/Midwest

First Printing in 2021.

To Tae and Lilja

... who are wise enough not to think too much
about the past or the future as they joyfully live their
childhoods today. Yesterday's stories will glow dimly
behind them, waiting patiently to flare up and illuminate
their lives when they are ready. And tomorrow's stories
will be revealed in their own time.

To Peggy McGrath Bailey

... who led me, when we were very young, into the magical
world of imagination.

And In Loving Remembrance of
Ann Werner Drazkowski

For so many years we wandered together side by side
through old cemeteries, listening to their hushed and
whispered tales.

Before his death, Judas Iscariot returned the thirty pieces of silver to high priests who had given them to him in exchange for betraying Jesus. But the priests did not return this "blood money" to the temple coffers. Instead, they used it to buy a field, later called a "potter's field," to bury strangers, criminals, and paupers. (Adapted from Matthew 27:3-27:8)

Preface

The Haunting of Potter's Field tells a series of mostly true stories about people buried in one Midwestern cemetery's potter's field. A potter's field was a burial place for the poor and the unclaimed. While these accounts come from one cemetery in Minnesota, they are representative of stories found in every potter's field in America. They help to tell America's story. A potter's field burial was free and marginal. Many graves had no head markers, at all. No one aspired to be buried in a potter's field. In the land of opportunity, it meant poverty, shame, and failure. But those notions were unfair. They did not tell the whole story.

These tales are not really ghost stories, although they do evoke the spirits of people long dead. They take us back to the late nineteenth and early twentieth centuries when earlier settlers, and native peoples who had been here for thousands of years, were inundated by newcomers, including newly arrived immigrants and others who were moving across the country, forming new towns along the way. Some were running away from trouble and scandal; most were simply seeking better lives.

Many people prospered ... but many did not. Despite their extraordinary efforts, some could not overcome the considerable challenges they faced. There was no social or financial safety net. Some people were alone, with families left behind in distant lands. Some people were illiterate or could not speak English. Some lost everything they had to unscrupulous con men. Many lacked marketable skills or suffered injuries or illnesses that limited their ability to work. Women and people of different ethnic backgrounds had to deal with prejudices and discrimination. And some people just had bad luck. When these people died, many were buried in potter's fields all across the country.

The Haunting of Potter's Field reimagines the lives of some brave, worthy people who were laid to rest in Woodlawn Cemetery's Potter's Field in Winona, Minnesota. All of them contributed to their community in unique and significant ways. The last of these tales is a compilation of several individuals' lives. The nineteenth and early twentieth century newspaper accounts, from which these stories were culled, may be the only records that these people ever lived. The stories are true to the extent that the newspaper accounts are true and I've imagined and developed them from there. The newspaper reporters probably spelled some unfamiliar names phonetically, and now there is no way to be sure of the actual names where they do not appear in census or other official records.

The Haunting of Potter's Field was originally written for the stage, as a performance piece. It featured actors, singers, dancers, and music by gifted local musicians and included original music by Brian Schellinger and Dr. Kelly McGuire. The basic rhyme scheme was chosen so that the stories could be simply and quickly told, keeping the stage action moving from one scene to the next.

I am happy to bring the stories of the struggles of these earlier Americans to life, so that we can all appreciate the price that some paid, and what it took to create this great country that we call home.

Margaret Shaw Johnson

The Haunting Of Potter's Field

Stories From The Past, Unearthed From The Grave

Margaret Shaw Johnson

Illustrated by
Jared Tuttle

Ravens Point Press

2021

Potter's Field

As I strode graveyard hill, something stopped me dead still,
'Midst the tumbled and crumbling stones.
A whispering chill gathered 'round me until,
Potter's field penetrated my bones!

Then the earth, parched and baked, darkly quivered and quaked,
Snaking fissures and rending the ground!
Vapors rose from the deep, spirits shaken from sleep,
Rose from sepulcher, gravesite and mound.

First they spoke with one tongue, mixed the old ones and young,
Moaning strangely and highly and low.
Sounds of islands of rain, sounds of poverty's strain,
Seeking all-where with nowhere to go.

"Don't Forget," was their cry, "though our memories die,
With our children, our labor, our dreams.
Crooked crosses mark years, flowers wilted with tears,
Potter's Field: it's more than it seems."

Then one voice breathed another, its sister, its brother,
A hundred, a hundred times ten.
The dead came alive, children, husbands and wives,
Do not fear them or spurn them again!

For here lie the plain folk, hard-hungered work-broke,
Who hammered and plastered and strained!
Who lifted and carried and sifted and ferried,
Who sickened and got up again.

Some came 'cross the sea, to breathe air fresh and free,
They were young, they were boisterous and loud!
Leaving families distraught, their hopes all for naught,
Left with sorrow, draped deep like a shroud.

Then my senses took flight, night was day, day was night,
Ghosts demanded I go where they led.
They emerged from the air—I'd been here, then went there,
In the past, I joined the undead.

Strangers In Our Midst!

(The Townfolk's Refrain)

All traveling west, the worst and the best,
Turned up here, then they left or else stayed.
They had stories to tell, from heaven or hell,
Turned us giddy, or glad or afraid.

For we couldn't be sure, when they said who they were,
No records to check and confirm.
Wearied man wants a job ... or to murder and rob?
'Round the hearth, we shared our concern.

The Hungarian Lord, who seemed stiff, proud and bored,
Had eyes shifty with cunning and stealth.
Nobility true, or a crook through and through,
On the run with another man's wealth?

"I'm a lady of means, seek a life of esteem."
- (She stole all he had while he slept!)
"I'm a gentleman true, here to start life anew."
- (Wife & children back home, vows unkept!)

All had secrets to hide, discarded pasts died,
And the secrets they kept deep inside.
Some were gentler folk, merely careworn and broke,
Bearing guilt as back home families cried.

Mister Foster

(d. 1893)

Mister Foster sold wares in the markets and fairs,
Thought we knew him for many a year.
Ne'er unburdened his mind of his past left behind,
Jokes and jollity buried his fear.

But his cares daily grew, and his friends never knew,
How worry robbed him of rest.
Then weary of strife, Foster ended his life,
His pain and his sins unconfessed.

We searched his trunk, his room and his bunk,
For money to bury him proud.
But his coffers were bare and we'd nothing to share.
He'd be doomed to a crude pauper's shroud.

Then came the night coach; I saw it approach,
As it screeched to a stop at the Inn.
A figure stepped down, dressed in black traveling gown,
Darkly veiled, yes, she must be his kin!

To assist her, I'd try, but she glided right by,
Scent of mystery left in her wake.
She was young, I could see, and she looked right through me.
Through black netting, I felt her heart break.

Then the young beauty cried, "I heard he has died!
Lay him not in a pauper's cold grave!
I could not bear to know, that his life ended so,
And his dignity I could not save!"

"Are you family, Ma'am? Have you come with a plan?
Have you means to inter him a'right?
Is 'Foster' his name? Tell us from whence he came!
Help us spare him this sorry plight!"

"Not kin, nor wife—one who loved him in life!
But I'm poor; I'm unable to pay!
Our names, I'll not give, secrets safe while I live,
Help me or I must hasten away!"

We looked all around, eyes cast guiltily down,
We'd no money to help the poor lass.
So she left as she came through the fog-heavy rain,
With her heartbreak, we watched the night pass.

Now a century's gone by, and still he does lie,
In a poor grave on Potter's Field hill.
The same damp cold rain, the same baffling refrain,
"Who was she? Who was he?" plagues us still.

Donald

(d. 1933)

He grinned at his hunch, as he skipped home for lunch,
That his ma had baked fresh apple pie.
He was seven, carefree, living life happily,
A gap-toothed, freckle-faced little guy.

Donald, his Pa, little brother and Ma,
Lived together down-road from the school.
Pa toiled for his pay, got them through day by day,
"Work hard and waste not" was their rule.

There was no time to swerve as it sped 'round the curve—
Little boy took the taxi cab's blow.
It was over so fast, Donald's short life had passed,
Leaving sorrow no family should know.

Parents wept, brother cried, their sweet Donald had died,
His gravesite must honor his life.
Potters' Field was free; thus a fine stone was key,
"He will have it!" Pa promised his wife.

So he bought it on time, every week paid a dime,
They installed it; engraved, it looked grand.
It helped just a bit, to take picnics and sit,
With their Donald, like holding his hand.

The Depression grew deep, Pa's debt burden, steep,
Missed payments, like losing his soul.
Bank said, "You'll not pay? Take that fine stone away!"
Wrenched it out of the earth, left a hole.

All his hope drained away, endless toiling each day,
His son was gone, life lost its light.
As he sank in despair, his youngest took care,
"I will help, Papa, let's make this right!"

So they gathered up sand, cement, all by hand,
Made a form from a broken-down crate.
Poured a slab, flat and thick, they inscribed with a stick,
Little Donald's initials and date.

In Potter's Field still, rests that slab on the hill,
With its memory of a small boy.
And a family's deep bond, 'til death and beyond,
They faced hardship with love, prayer and joy.

Wah-A-Hauga

(d. 1907)

We called him "Joe Hall," not his name, not at all,
'Twas "Wah-A-Hauga," proud native son.
As he traveled to town, the train struck him down,
With his tenure as chief just begun.

The elders were wise, "Daughter, let us advise:
Lay him here, in our hallowed land,
As our fathers before, 'neath the trees, by the shore!"
But his daughter had something else planned.

Her unusual request deemed the town graveyard best,
So grieved family and kin gathered round.
With no money to pay, tattered clothing a'fray
They pondered hard Potter's Field ground.

Then bearing his pine box, slipping on wet rocks,
They struggled up steep Potter's Hill.
Jim Blackhawk, afore, trailed by fifteen and more,
As the townsfolk stood back, keeping still.

At the top, Blackhawk kneeled, dropped the lid in the field,
So their lost one once more knew the air,
Chanted songs from the ages, intoned words of sages,
Tobacco, they laced through his hair.

Then off in a sleigh, family bundled away,
Silence, Wah-A-Hauga's only knell.
Up the river they went, brother's soul rightly sent,
As the night and the snow softly fell.

When the days lengthened long, spring birds sang their song,
And the grief the clan felt turned to hope,
Turned to planting and life, purging winter's long strife,
Sun's heat made it easier to cope.

Then the people came out from the valleys about,
The tribes danced with ghosts of the Fox.
Their laughter and song raised a rhythmic throng,
To welcome the spring equinox.

The Pest House

As I pondered the scene, a mist grayly-green,
Gathered ominously, rising below.
My arms covered my head; creeping fingers of dread,
Showed a horse, draped black buggy in tow.

As the rig rumbled near, I shrank back in fear,
Its passengers: Sickness, Despair.
Pest House in the clearing ... quarantine with death nearing!
These may die, for the others they'll care.

Diseases abounding, their symptoms compounding,
Yellow fever, consumption and flu,
Cholera, phrenitis, smallpox, appendicitis,
And the doctors and treatments too few.

So they shut them away in the Pest House to stay,
All alone in a dark, distant place.
In that shed in the wood, pious nurses do good,
Live or die? Left to God and His grace.

Mister Rich

(d. 1893)

"Rich" was not his real name, when he came on the train,
From the East, with his grip and his plan.
Lived among us as neighbors, did the town lots of favors,
People loved him, a capital man!

But he did like his fun, liked the beer, gin and rum,
Quick to anger, he riled the wrong man.
It started a brawl, shots rang out, caused his fall!
"Bind the wound! Save Rich if we can!"

"'Tweren't me!" snarled McFee, "Rich shot first! Set me free!
Ask this lot, they'll swear just as I said!"
And he glared at the crowd, muttered threats, some out loud,
Cross this man and you'll find yourself dead.

McFee went to jail, while Rich, weak and pale,
Lay a-bed and he might not survive.
"Take his statement!" they said, "'fore the trial, he'll be dead!
He must testify while he's alive!"

So the judge came around and they wrote it all down,
Rich, unarmed, was shot in the back!
So he swore, so he'd sign, McFee guilty of crime,
Rich the victim of fatal attack!

With the statement now signed, Rich grew weak and resigned,
It was sad, he would soon be deceased.
His people should know ... who to write, where to go?
"Give your name!" urged the judge and the priest.

But they couldn't compel, and he never did tell—
Said his dear mother must never know,
Of his poor desperate end, he'd not grieve her again.
Potter's Field's unmarked grave laid him low.

So the crook went to trial, slouching sloven and vile,
Witnesses silenced by fear, shock and dread ...
Save one with no name, from his grave did lay blame!
Villain doomed by the words of the dead.

Ye Fun

(d. 1876)

Ye Fun was a son of the Celestial Kingdom,
As China was known in that day.
He sailed 'cross the sea, with his friend, Yep Yelly,
They'd find work that their fortunes would pay!

The West Coast came in view. They cheered; spirits flew!
They'd be rich, they were saved, they'd find gold!
But in time it was clear, they faced violence and fear.
"No Chinese! No work here!" they were told.

They talked it all through, just two jobs left to do,
Start a restaurant or wash other's clothes.
But they'd move further east, Minnesota, at least.
Start a laundry and see how it goes!

Among us they found space, started in at a pace,
Hard work earned their place in the town.
And as business grew, kinsmen came, quite a few!
Turned our standards of "clean" upside down!

They wilted in steam, hot irons pressed a seam,
Their hands blistered raw from lye suds.
They laundered with care and their prices were fair,
Crisp shirts, ruffled skirts and clean duds!

One day before dawn, Ye Fun rose, looking wan,
But he rallied, felt fine, so he said.
Then a tragic surprise, when before his friend's eyes,
Ye Fun gasped, grabbed his chest and fell dead!

All the purse he had earned, he'd to China returned,
Hungry parents, a family of ten.
"Naught for a grave ... Potter's Field, funds will save!"
Thought the anguished Chinese laundry men.

Still they honored the old ways and harkened by-gone days,
They summoned the past as they grieved.
First Chinese rites on this soil, marking Ye Fun's long toil,
Ancient rituals soothed the bereaved.

Dusk descended that day when they gathered to pray,
Hoisted parcels and started to go.
An oil lamp held high, as stars twinkled the sky,
Chinese laundrymen, all in a row.

Through tall grasses they went, to the graveside event.
Filled the tomb with soft earth halfway up.
Built a fire, burned his clothes, his goods and his robes,
Laid a feast, shared a ritual cup.

For Ye Fun, they left rice, boiled eggs cut up twice,
With lard slices on either side.
Raw potatoes regaled, with wood spears impaled,
The grave filled, they left him with pride.

Years left him behind, though no peace did he find,
Ye Fun's bones rested restless and pained.
Ghostly voices invaded, would not be dissuaded,
"Left your homeland, ancestors remained!"

Yep Yelly heard it too. He knew what to do,
He must restore tranquility.
So he dug up the bones; he would take the bones home,
On a voyage once more 'cross the sea.

We watched them depart, two friends heart-to-heart,
Toward that same leaky ship in the night.
Yep Yelly, not alone, as he cradled the bones,
Wrapped in linen, scrubbed clean and bleached white.

Old Mose

(d. 1928)

Old Mose was a codger, a revenue dodger,
Who wandered the streets of our town.
With no proper home, our alleys he'd roam,
Hawking treasures that grew in the ground.

He scoured the woodlands, with skilled eye and deft hands,
Found mushrooms, the common and rare.
Mixed in stroganoff, earthy stew, rich brown broth,
Mose's mushrooms were our special fare.

On a cold autumn day, Billy Bronk went to play,
With his friend 'neath the town's eastern hill.
Saw a squalid old shack, at first fear held them back,
When the moaning grew pained, loud and shrill.

Found Mose looking poor, crumbled weak on the floor,
To the doctor, a hospital bed!
There he lingered a spell, he had stories to tell,
The boys listened to all that he said.

Started off with a smile, then he coughed for a while,
Sputtered, "Boys, if you'd known me when!
I was famous, you see, oh, the WONDER of me!
Ah, those days, I would live them again!

"I've a musical soul, on the stage I'd a role,
As HERNANDO, THE VAUDEVILLE STAR!
'Oh, please lead our show, the world's best, you know!'
Begged Ringling, the brash Circus Czar!"

"But I had my own troupe, a jolly old group,
With acrobats, actors and band!
We sang for our bread, drank too much, lost our head,
Every town filled a tent, it was grand!"

"Dusty roads through the West, tambourines, songs and jest!
We were happy, 'though ragged and broke.
Then one day it was gone, Vaudeville lost its song,
Magic vagabond life up in smoke."

So Mose ended up here, foraging with the deer,
HERNANDO, THE VAUDEVILLE STAR!
His last nickel was spent, money lost, money lent,
Bumming drinks from the guys at the bar.

When he died, few to mourn, 'cause some held him in scorn,
Laid him down in a stark pauper's grave.
And in time most forgot that he'd lived, lived a lot,
And the music and song that he gave.

But when came summer's end, Billy went with his friend,
To his grave, talked of life on the roam.
Then ... the mushrooms rose up—fleshy white, rosy cup!
They would sell them when they got back home!

And sell them, they did; housewives lifted the lid,
Of the simmering Mushroom Pot Stew.
Breathed the heady, rich scent earthy mushroom caps lent,
Reminding them of You Know Who!

Now, mushrooms, you know, are just fungi that grow,
On loamy soil rich with decay.
Their complexity fed, by things that are dead,
Plants and fauna, dissolving away.

So Mose had the last joke, on those haughty townsfolk,
Folks who scorned him and looked down their nose.
They enjoyed every bite, gourmet Vaudeville Delight,
Grave top treats, sprouted right from his toes!

Joey Brom

(d. 1901)

Joey Brom was fifteen, oldest son of Maxine,
And Ernest, who'd died at the mill.
With a houseful to feed, and the family in need,
No more school now, a man's role to fill.

So he worked every day, no more time now for play.
Still, he longed for an easier road.
After work, in the dark, walked the streets, past the park,
Dreaming dreams that would lessen his load.

'Long the broad avenue, where the houses were few,
Of the wealthy, the town's genteel class,
Lights gaily glowed, couples danced, champagne flowed,
Joey watched, through the fogged window glass.

"What have they," he thought, "that my family has not?
They own banks, we have nothing to save.
Wrapped in luxury's grace, they sleep warm, in soft lace,
While my pa lies in Potter's Field grave!"

He thought it all through, made his plans, notions grew,
Went from sweeper to foreman to boss,
Put aside all he could, others wouldn't; he would.
Then he learned of the owner's dread loss!

So he gathered his stash, bought the factory with cash,
And he rose to the top like the cream.
Grand home and wife, pampered children, fine life,
Lived and loved the American Dream!

But then came the day his son, Abe, moved away,
To the East, first for school then for good.
Built a prosperous life, made an heiress his wife.
He looked forward, not back, as one should.

In time Abe grew old, but the stories he told,
By the hearth, to his children and theirs!
Tales of great grandpa Joe, the Midwest he'd loved so,
Family history passed down to his heirs.

Thus, lured by the past, Abe's grandson came, at last,
To that homeland to seek out his roots.
Distinguished and staid, Eastern gent finely made,
Strode the graveyard in soft handmade boots.

Midst the angels of stone, he admired, alone,
The tombs of the city's elite.
Joey's obelisk rose high, granite gleamed, pierced the sky,
Modeling taste, elegant and discreet.

He sat down, swelled with pride. His forefathers died,
Blessed with money, position, and skill!
Didn't see Potter's Field in the distance revealed,
Where lay Ernest ... who'd died at the mill.

The Spirits Retreat

Then I woke in the field, and I knew I must yield,
To the gathering dark and the chill.
Knew my family was waiting, the specters were fading,
But they whispered, persistently, still.

"Don't forget us!" they said, "though we're many years dead,
We struggled so hard to prevail!
We left you our rules, our talents and tools,
We fought against every travail.

"So use those gifts well, and our stories, do tell,
Know your good life did not start with you!
Live it well and with heart, pass it on, do your part,
Honor us; yours will honor you, too."

Then the field lost its din and a calm settled in,
The turmoil and anguish did cease.
Their time now to rest, they had given their best,
"Take our love, gently rest now in peace."

The Haunting Of Potter's Field
"Tell Your Story"

Brian Schellinger

If you should find yourself in Pot-ter's Field, and the mys-tic a – air makes your

sen – ses reel and an ap – par – i – tion sud–den – ly lends a face to a name

You're wondring who was lost who was saved when these spir–its rise right

out of the grave Did you shake and shi–ver or stand and de–li–ver nobod–y knows.

No – bod – y knows til they're wear in' a dead man's

clothes. Oh!

Tell your sto – ry Tell your sto – ry

What left you wan – der–ing and want – ing too?

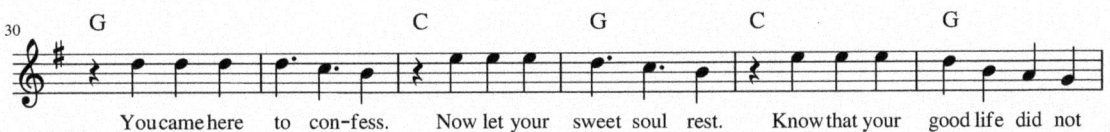

You came here to con-fess. Now let your sweet soul rest. Know that your good life did not

end — — — — with you.

2nd Verse:

Was there no time for the plans you made..the ones you held so dear on this earthly plane,
And did you draw your last breath, knowing death made the circle of life?
Why did you feel the need to set the record straight? When the moment came and you met your fate,
No time to borrow, no tomorrow, nobody knows.
Nobody knows 'til they're wearin' a dead man's clothes. Oh!

Chorus:

Tell your story! Tell your story! What left you wandering and wanting too?
You came here to confess. Now, let your sweet soul rest.
Know that your good life did not end..with you.

"Maggie's Lament"

Kelly McGuire

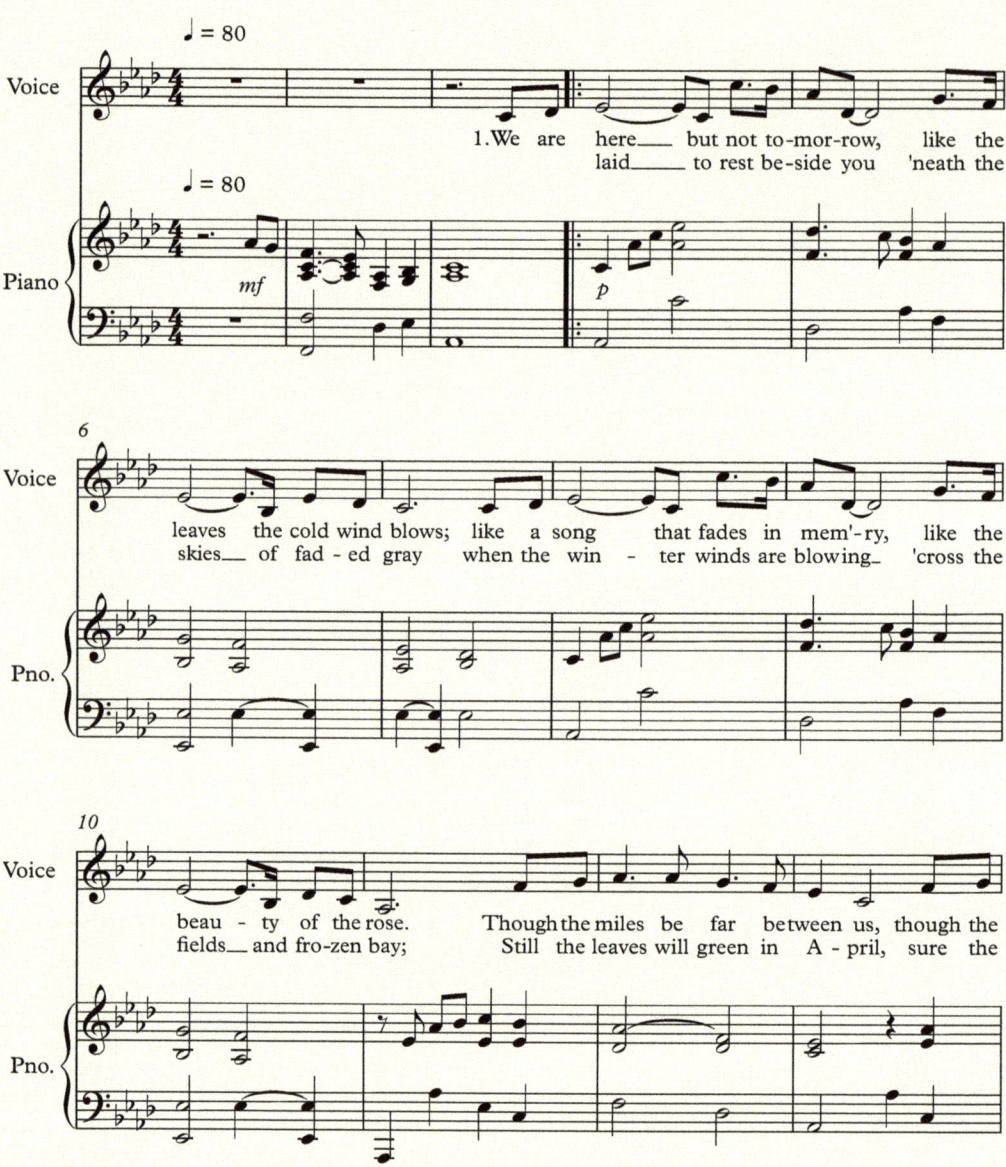

1. We are here___ but not to-mor-row, like the
laid___ to rest be-side you 'neath the

leaves the cold wind blows; like a song___ that fades in mem'-ry, like the
skies___ of fad - ed gray when the win - ter winds are blow ing___ 'cross the

beau - ty of the rose. Though the miles be far be-tween us, though the
fields___ and fro-zen bay; Still the leaves will green in A - pril, sure the

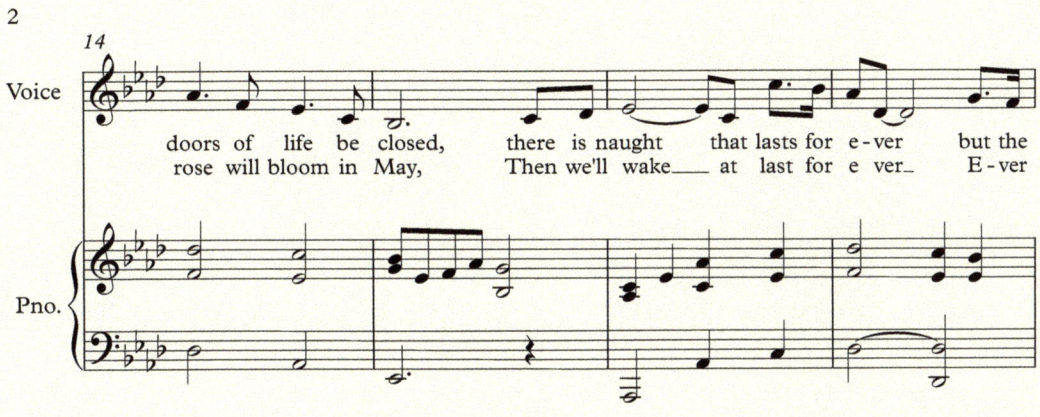

doors of life be closed,   there is naught   that lasts for e - ver   but the
rose will bloom in May,   Then we'll wake___ at last for e ver___   E - ver

love___   my true one   knows.
more___   in love's new   day.

2.I'll be

Biographies

Margaret Shaw Johnson served as a District Court Judge in Minnesota's Third Judicial District for twenty-one years before dedicating herself to honing her skills as an author and a playwright. She focuses on finding true, but largely unknown, stories from history and bringing them to life on the page and on the stage. Inquiries about this book or the script for *The Haunting of Potters Field* and other works by Margaret Shaw Johnson may be sent to Ravens Point Press at ravenspointpress@gmail.com.

Jared Tuttle, a graduate of the Minneapolis College of Art and Design, is a freelance illustrator and designer who specializes in illustration, branding and packaging. His style is diverse, ranging from classical influences to magical realism and anything in between and beyond. Jared can be reached at hello@jared-tuttle.com.

Rachel Tesch Hudachek is a Graphic Designer and graduate of the Minneapolis College of Art and Design. She is an eclectic designer who enjoys working on a wide variety of projects. When she is not working she is watching Youtube, researching unexplained phenomena, and crushing her friends at video games. Rachel can be reached at rachelltesch@gmail.com.

Brian Schellinger is a latter-day troubadour. He is a singer, songwriter, poet, musician, and actor. He has entertained for audiences of all ages across the USA and Canada. Brian is also known affectionately as "Uncle Squaty" for his nationally acclaimed recordings for early childhood education, utilized by teachers all over the world. Inquiries can be sent to squatyboy@live.com.

Kelly McGuire started playing piano as a small child. He went on to study a variety of instruments and obtained a degree in music performance from Winona State University. Then he moved to his left brain and pursued a career in medicine. He practiced Internal Medicine in northeastern Wisconsin for twenty-five years. Since retiring Kelly has returned to his first love of music and has continued to write, perform and record music in several genres. He volunteers with the free local clinic and St. Vincent de Paul Society. Kelly can be reached at kmcguire@svdpmarinette.com.

Many Thanks

I am grateful to the many people who helped me place these long-forgotten stories into a proper historical and social context and to create this book. My primary source materials were contemporary newspaper accounts, written by white reporters who were people of their own time with their own cultural biases. To better understand the story of Ye Fun I was assisted by Bingwen Yan, President of the Alliance of Minnesota Chinese Organizations, Josephine Lee, Professor of English and Asian American Studies at the University of Minnesota, and Pearl Bergad, Executive Director of the Chinese Heritage Foundation. I learned a lot from Erika Lee and her book *The Making of Asian America: A History*. I am grateful to Sherri Gebert Fuller and her book *Chinese In Minnesota: The People of Minnesota*, published by the Minnesota Historical Society. None of these people purport to speak for their organizations or the entire Chinese American community but their insights and counsel were very helpful.

I sought information and the advice of people of the Ho Chunk Nation. It is my hope that Wah-A-Hauga's story, as written, honors their people, their culture, and their history. And I am grateful to the now-deceased Harvey Brossard, who told me the story of his family and his brother, Donald.

Converting a work created for the stage to one that works on the page is no small task. Heartfelt thanks to Jared Tuttle, whose luminous illustrations bring the work to life, and to Rachel Tesch Hudachek, interior book designer, for her excellent work. Thanks to Brian Schellinger and Kelly McGuire for allowing me to publish their music! My gratitude to editor Sandy Sullivan of Ivywild Editing and Writing Services, and to the very knowledgeable Rachel Anderson of RMA Publicity.

My writer, artist, and theater friends were a big help to me: Lynn Nankivil, Ken McCullough, Kathy and Greg Peterson, Emilio DeGrazia, Jeanne and Paul Skattum, Patrick Ledray, Fran Edstrom, Judy Myers, Melissa Maxwell, Benjamin Bouchvalt, Anne Scott Plummer, and Shelly Olson, former owner of the independent bookstore Paperbacks and Pieces. And I am grateful for my long-term, reliable friends: Peggy McGrath Bailey, Laurie Lucas, Enid Underdahl, Carolyn McGuire, Loretta Frederick, Kim Foster, David Schreiber, and Taff Roberts.

Finally, thanks to my sons, Hans and Aran and their wives, and to my story-loving grandchildren, Tae and Lilja! My brothers, Bob and Richard Shaw and their families are a loving presence in my life as is my sister-in-law Midge Shaw, her family, and the whole, extended Johnson clan especially Gail Huschle, an astute observer of human nature. Most of all, I thank my husband, Bruce Johnson, who suffers with me through all the doubts and bad times, who rejoices in my successes and who is ever constant in his love and support.

This work begins and ends at Woodlawn, the beautiful nineteenth-century park cemetery in Winona, Minnesota, the slumbering place of thousands of stories just waiting to be awakened. Thanks to the Woodlawn cast and crew, and to the folks at the Winona County and Minnesota historical societies who help me ferret out information and learn about the history that I love.

Margaret Shaw Johnson